First American Paperback Edition, 1999

First American Edition 1986 by Kane/Miller Book Publishers
Brooklyn, New York & La Jolla, California

Originally published in Japan in 1984 under the title
Yukinko by Fukutake Publishing Co., Ltd., Tokyo, Japan

Copyright © Masako Hidaka

American text copyright © 1986 Kane/Miller Book Publishers

Library of Congress Cataloging-in-Publication Data

Hidaka, Masako.
Girl from the snow country.
Translation of: Yukinko.
Summary: A little Japanese girl enjoys the falling snow as
she makes snow bunnies and walks across the snowy fields
with her mother to the village market.
[1. Snow—Fiction. 2. Japan—Fiction] I. Title.
PZ7.H53164Gi   1986   [E]   86-10584

ISBN 0-916291-93-6
Printed and bound in Singapore by Tien Wah Press Pte. Ltd.
1 2 3 4 5 6 7 8 9 10

Girl From The Snow Country

By Masako Hidaka

Translated by Amanda Mayer Stinchecum

A   C R A N K Y   N E L L   B O O K

 **KM** Kane/Miller Book Publishers

Brooklyn, New York & La Jolla, California

The snow falls steadily, burying mountains and rice fields in silence, piling up on the persimmon tree in the garden.

Each winter snow blankets Mi-chan's village.

Day and night, the snow kept falling,
until it was *this* deep! Tama the cat, who
hates the cold, sat staring at the snow while . . .

. . . Mi-chan put on her boots and stepped down into the garden.

The snow was soft and fluffy. Crouching down
quietly on the drifts, she noticed some small round
clumps of snow.

"I know what I'll do!" she said, and, picking
leaves from a nearby camellia bush, she stuck two
into each white clump of snow.

"Look! Snow bunnies! But there's something wrong," she thought. "They should have red eyes."

As Mi-chan wondered how to fix them, Mommy called, "Do you want to go marketing with me?"

"Let's go!" Mi-Chan called back. And as she stood up, a small bird perched on a bare tree flew up into the air, shaking the snow from the branches and crying peep. . . . peep. . . . peep.

Mi-chan and Mommy walked along, treading on the pure white snow. Mommy's boots went crunch crunch, while Mi-chan's went squeak squeak across the silent snowfields.

After they had walked awhile, they came upon a stone statue of Jizo, protector of children and travelers, who was cloaked in snow.

"Jizo must be cold too, covered with all that snow," Mommy said.

"Well, I'll just brush it off for him," said Mi-chan, as she swept off the snow that had piled up on Jizo's head and shoulders.

Ahead of them the stalls of the morning market appeared. Inside the stalls, the market women were selling all kinds of things.

The first stall sold dolls made of rice flour,
and there were many rice-flour dogs on display.

"Let's buy a cute little dog! We can stick it
in front of the house," said Mi-chan.

"That's a good idea," her Mommy answered.
"He'd drive away any nasty demons around,
wouldn't he?"

So Mommy bought a big dog, and Mi-chan
bought a little one.

Next door was a fish stand, with crabs and shrimp heaped up in wooden crates along with the fish. Mommy picked out some crabs for a special treat.

While Mommy was buying the crabs,
Mi-chan took a peek at the next stall.
"Do you want some flowers, little girl?"
the flower lady asked.

Mi-chan, suddenly remembering her snow rabbits, replied, "At home I made these snow bunnies. I wanted to put eyes on them, but I couldn't find anything to use. What do you think I should do?"

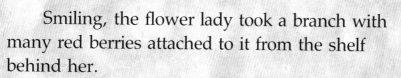

Smiling, the flower lady took a branch with
many red berries attached to it from the shelf
behind her.

"How about these?" she asked.

"They're just right. But how much are they?"
Mi-chan wanted to know.

"Since you're so sweet, you can have them
for free. Run home now and put eyes on
your snow bunnies," the flower lady said.

She broke off a branch loaded with berries and
handed it to Mi-chan.

"Well, thank you," said Mi-chan.

"Come back again soon," the flower lady said.

Holding the branch of red berries with great care,
Mi-chan started out for home with Mommy. On
the way, Mi-chan told her about the snow rabbits.

As they neared the statue of Jizo,
Mommy said to her, "You brushed
the snow off Jizo, so he helped you
find what you wanted."

Mi-chan and Mommy bowed their
heads in thanks before Jizo.

As soon as Mi-chan got home, she put
eyes on her snow rabbits with the red berries
she had brought. They looked as if they were
about to hop away, just like real rabbits.

"Mommy! Mommy! I finished my snow
bunnies!" said Mi-chan excitedly.

"How nice," Mommy's voice called out
from the kitchen.

The snow, which begins to fall again, drifts steadily, silently down, piling up on the snow rabbits.